The Musical Mice And Their Great Adventure

Deneen Kirsch – Gambrell

Illustrated by

Betty L. Grummer

AuthorHouse™
1663 Liberty Drive
Bloomington, IN 47403
www.authorhouse.com
Phone: 1-800-839-8640

Published by AuthorHouse 05/06/2013

ISBN: 978-1-4817-4855-1 (sc)
978-1-4817-4854-4 (e)

Library of Congress Control Number: 2013908133

Any people depicted in stock imagery provided by Thinkstock are models,
and such images are being used for illustrative purposes only.
Certain stock imagery © Thinkstock.

This book is printed on acid-free paper.

author**HOUSE**®

This book is dedicated to my wonderful mother, Norma Jean Kirsch. She has given me her love and support my entire life. Thank you, Mom. I love you, and I hope you enjoy this funny little book.

This book is a sequel to the book No Music for Mouseville.

Old King Rob had a wonderful life.
He rules a land filled with musical
mice.

4

Every day King Rob was delighted
to hear
The performing arts of his mice so
dear.

One day a surprise made King Rob's day.

Word came from the Queen from a land far away.

The musical mice were to play for the Queen.

Such excitement had never been seen!

They packed all their instruments, and boarded the ship.

They hoped this voyage would be a nice trip.

8

Excited mice scrambled all over the place.
They couldn't have gone faster if running a race.

The mice watched the whales jump
out of the sea.
They even saw coconuts up in a
tree.

10

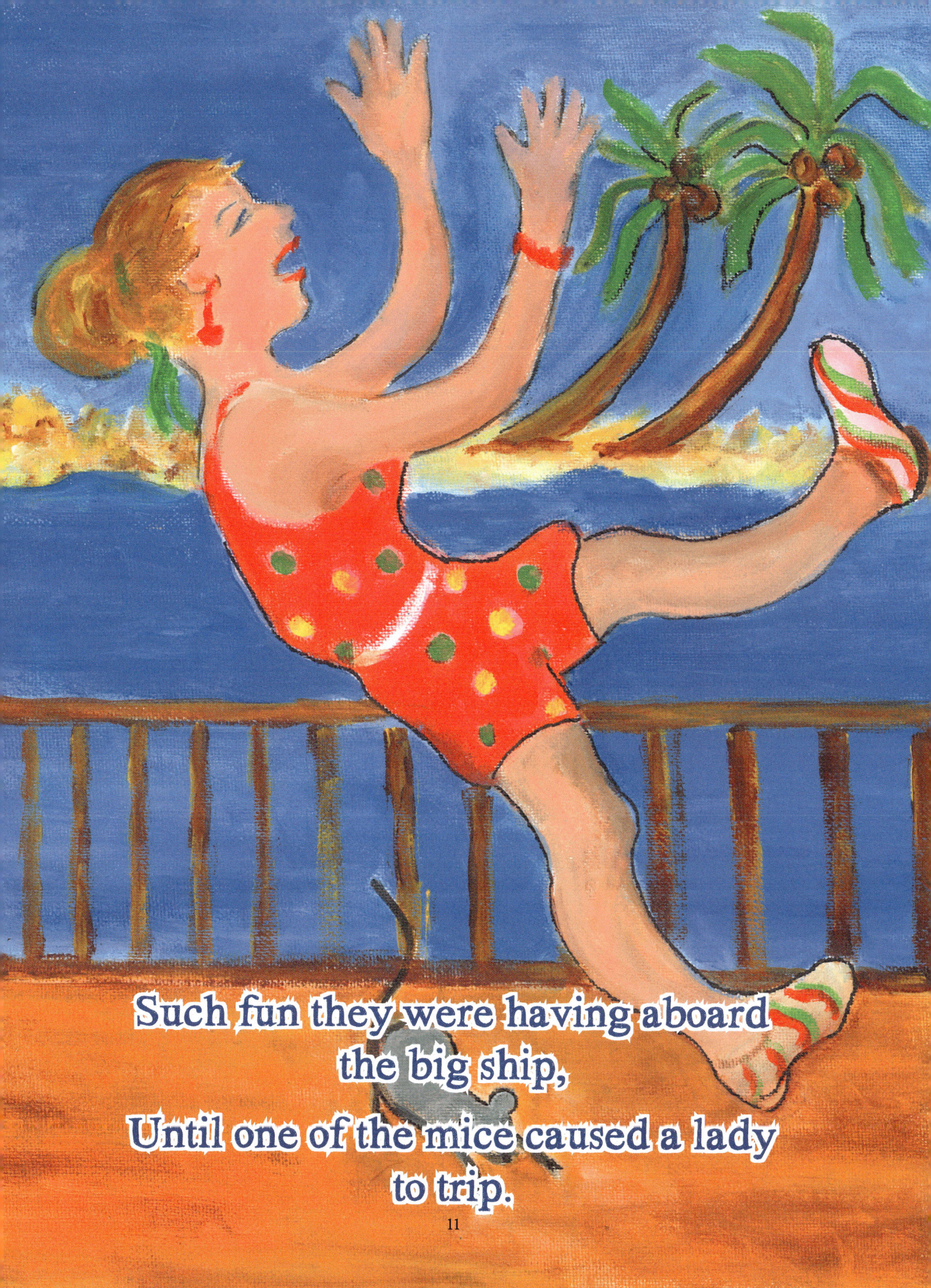

Such fun they were having aboard
the big ship,
Until one of the mice caused a lady
to trip.

11

After nearly falling, she sat down to rest.

Then the lady screamed "EEEEEEKKKKKK!!!" these rodents are pests.

Chef Joe shook his spoon, and chef
Moe took a knife!
The piano mouse barely escaped
with her life!

Sadly the mice decided to hide,
In the belly of the ship for the rest of the ride.

Once safely docked and the ship
was clear
King Rob asked to see Queen
Guinevere.

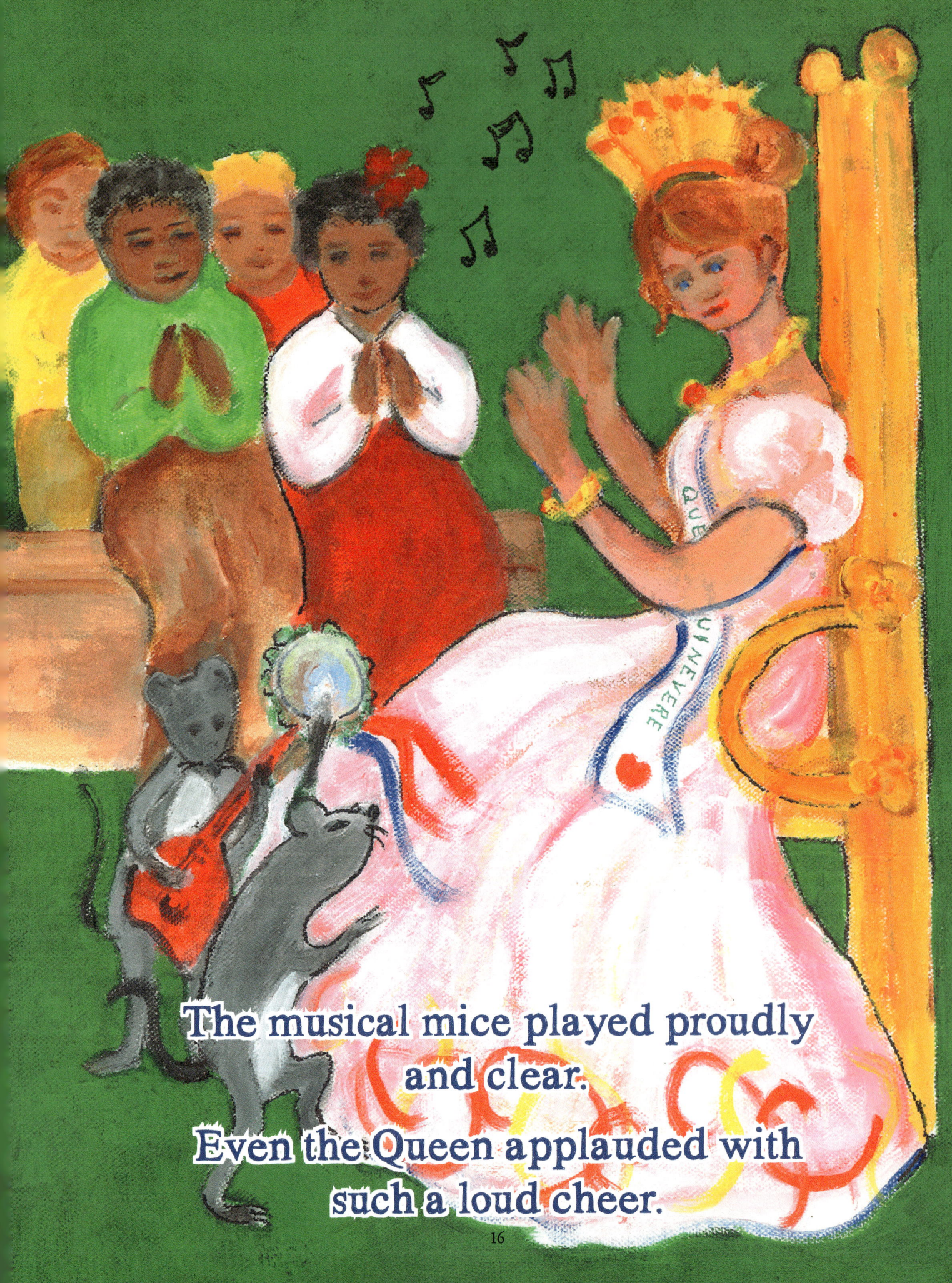

The musical mice played proudly
and clear.

Even the Queen applauded with
such a loud cheer.

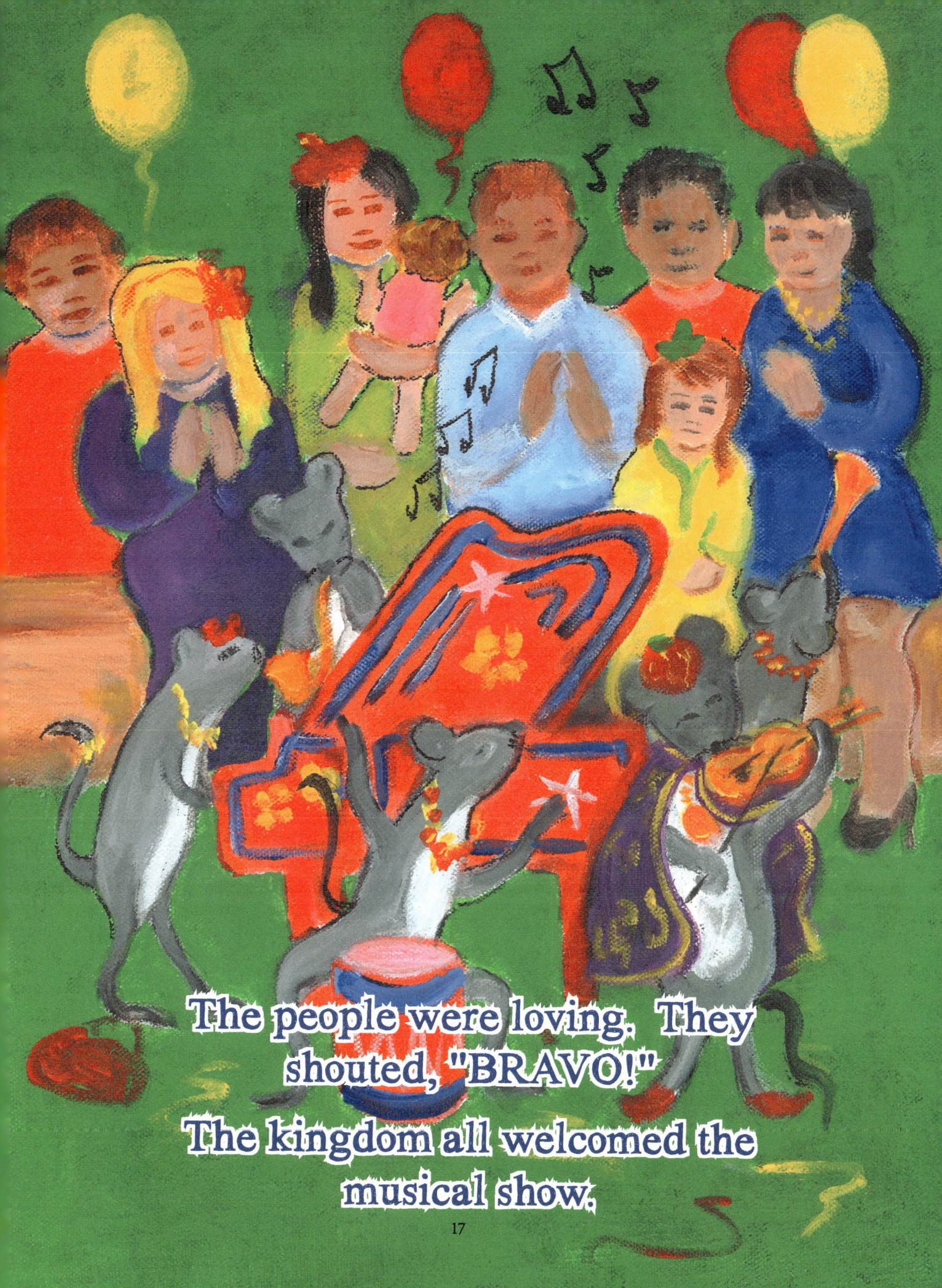

The people were loving. They shouted, "BRAVO!"

The kingdom all welcomed the musical show.

17

The cooks on the boat heard a booming, "BRAVO!"

Quite to the surprise of Chef Joe and Chef Moe.

18

The Musical Mice they had chased before,
were the cause of the clapping and deafening roar.

Then another surprise came out of
the blue

The ship's Captain had an
announcement, too.

20

Captain Stan said, "On the
returning trip,
These Musical Mice will perform on
my ship."

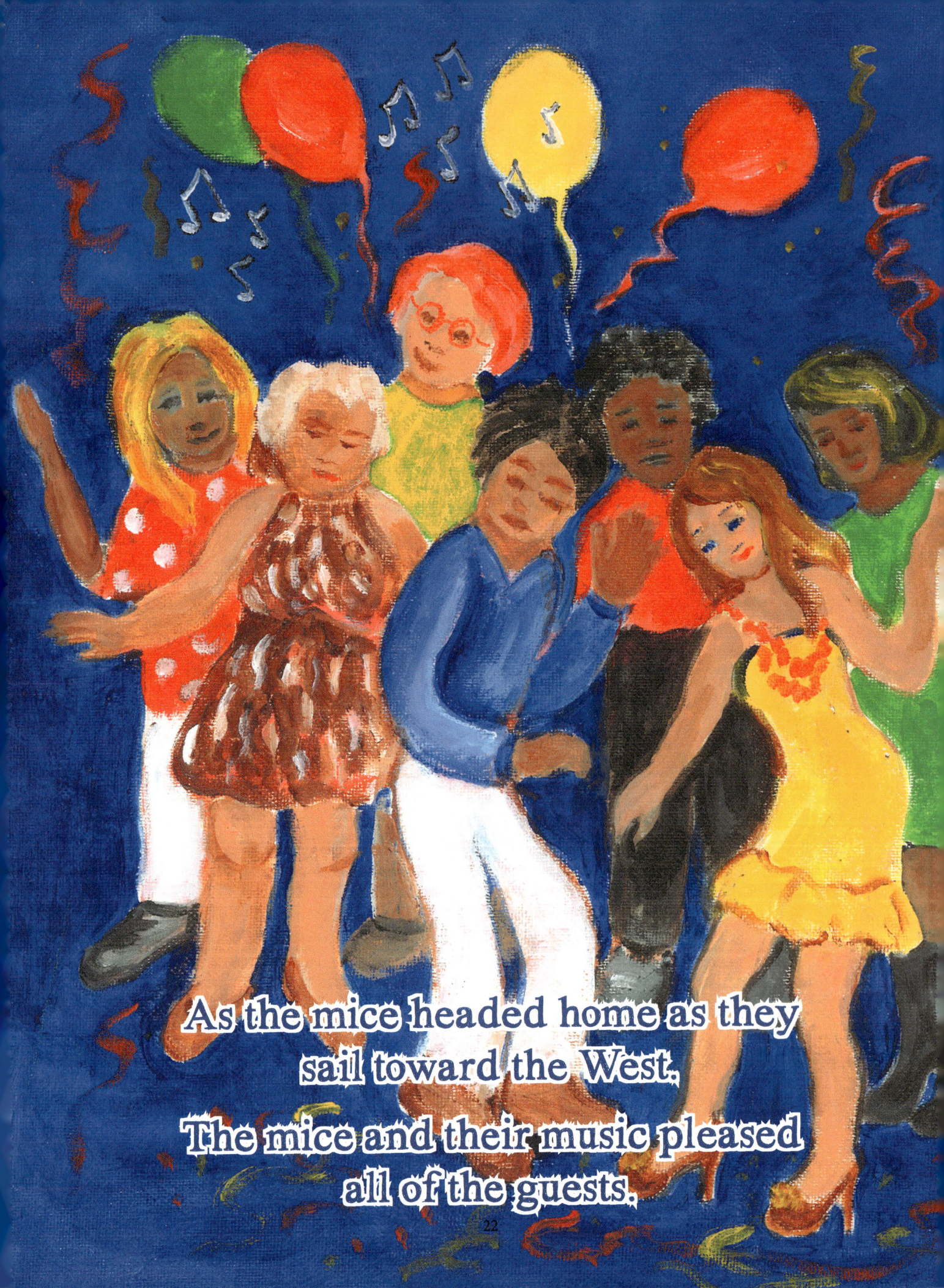

As the mice headed home as they
sail toward the West.

The mice and their music pleased
all of the guests.

MOUSEVILLE →

The passengers danced, and all wanted more.

But the ship sadly docked, the mice headed for shore.

23

King Rob and his mice loved the
Musical Trip
Oh the stories they'd tell about the
adventurous ship.

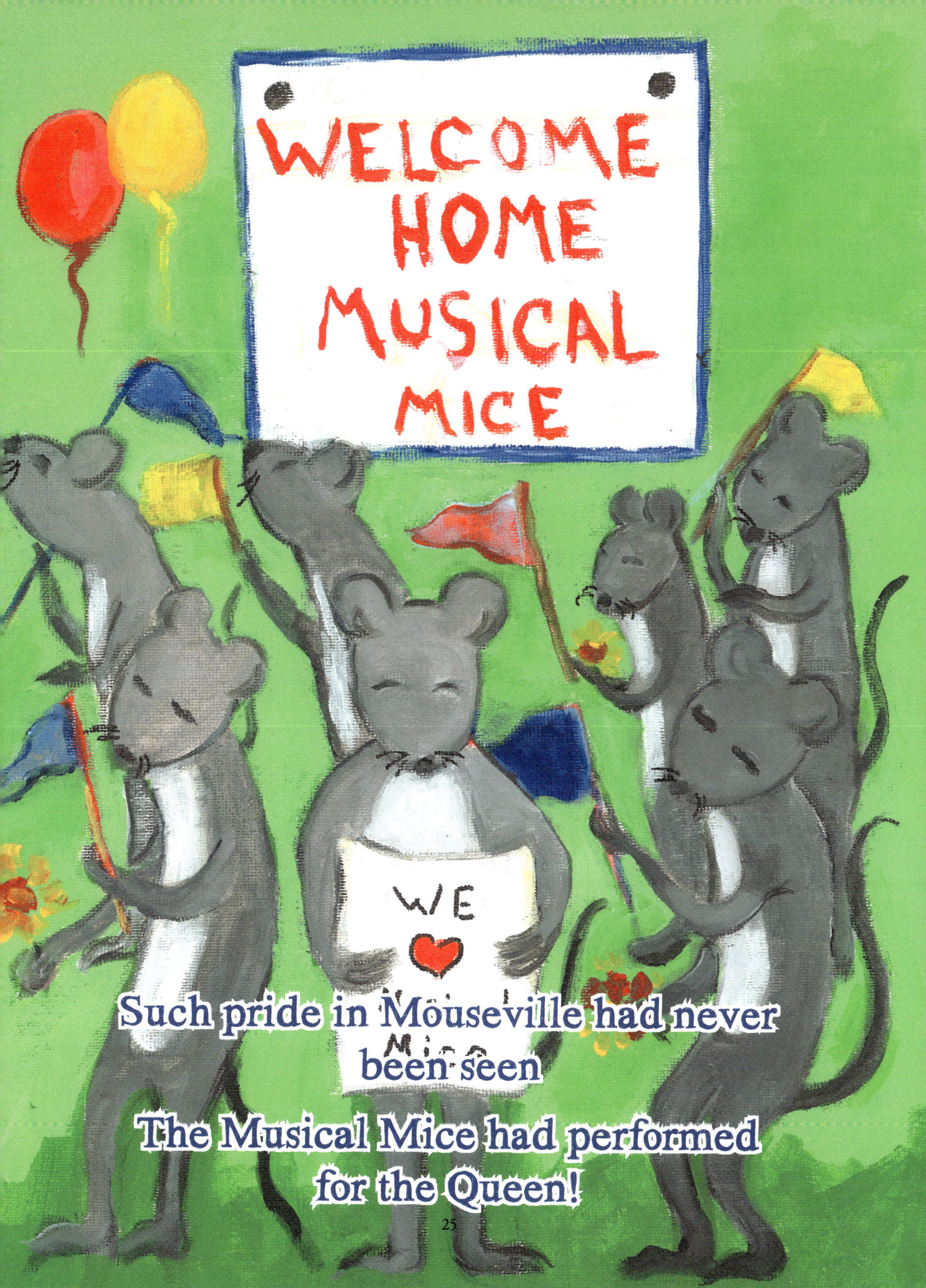

Such pride in Mouseville had never been seen

The Musical Mice had performed for the Queen!

CPSIA information can be obtained
at www.ICGtesting.com
Printed in the USA
LVIC061939130513
333603LV00001B